CAMY BAKER'S

love you like
a sister

30 cool rules for making and being a better best friend

Other Skylark Books you will enjoy
Ask your bookseller for the books you have missed

Anne of Green Gables by L. M. Montgomery
Horse Crazy, The Saddle Club #1 by Bonnie Bryant
The Great Mom Swap by Betsy Haynes
The Great Dad Disaster by Betsy Haynes
Breaking the Ice, Silver Blades #1 by Melissa Lowell
Pronounce It Dead by Ivy Ruckman
Elvis Is Back, and He's in the Sixth Grade!
by Stephen Mooser

Camy Baker's

love you like a sister

30 cool rules for making and being a better best friend

A SKYLARK BOOK

New York • Toronto • London • Sydney • Auckland

RL 5.0, 009–012

CAMY BAKER'S LOVE YOU LIKE A SISTER

A Bantam Skylark Book / September 1998

ISBN 0-553-48656-X

Published simultaneously in the United States and Canada.

PRINTED IN THE UNITED STATES OF AMERICA

OPM   0   9   8   7   6   5   4   3

a note from camy baker

hey, girls!

My name is Camy Baker, and I'm what you might call an expert on friendship. Why? Because I used to go to Beverly Hills Elementary, one of the toughest schools in the country in terms of making friends.

I'm a sixth grader at Peoria Middle School right now. If you don't know where Peoria is, it's a really great city in Illinois.

It's a lot colder in Illinois than sunny Southern California. But I like the cold weather. I get to wear all my really *FIERCE* thrift store sweaters! ☺

While I miss my friends in Beverly Hills very much, I must admit it was easier for me to fit into my new school. The reason: Kids in Peoria are more down-to-earth. I think it's because the kids in Beverly Hills came from families that had a *lot* of money. When kids have a lot of money, there's pressure on them to act, dress, and think a certain way.

Sometimes not having a lot of money is a good thing. I know, I know. You're thinking, "Is she crazy?! I'd take mo' money any day!" But after living in Beverly Hills, I know money is *not* the key to happiness.

Oh, sure, the rich kids had the best clothes, took really exotic vacations with their parents, and lived in incredible homes. But were they *happy*? It depends. Usually the happiest girls I knew were the ones who had really good friendships.

If you want to know the truth, the happiest people I know *anywhere* are the ones who have really good friendships.

Besides family, the most important people you will ever have in your life are friends. Friends are the people who will help you celebrate the good times—and friends will also help you through the bad ones.

Having a really incredible friendship is about

the best thing that can happen to you. If you understand this, I guarantee your life will be *very* wonderful!

Love You Like a Sister was inspired by all the great friends I've made in Beverly Hills and Peoria. My friends have taught me so much about the world, and most importantly, about *myself*.

Since friendships are so important in our lives, I wanted to come up with *the* perfect thirty cool rules for making and being a better best friend.

Then I thought, "Camy, you have all these incredible friends. Why don't you get rules from them, too!"

So that's exactly what I did. I asked some of my closest pals to help me out with the rules. They were all really excited and helpful. After all, what are friends for? ☺

Before I move on to the first rule, I want to briefly tell you about the girls you'll be meeting later in the book.

I have to start with my best friend, Jackie O'Leary. Jackie's a crazy girl and I love her so much! She has really wild red hair. She's hilarious and brave and outrageous, and she talks almost as much as I do! When we're together chattering away, it can get a little crazy!

You're also going to meet Rachel. (I can't tell you what Rachel's last name is. Rachel's mother is a very famous movie star and Rachel likes to keep her last name secret.)

Rachel was my best friend in Beverly Hills and we're still very close. She's currently traveling around the world with her mother, and she has her own personal tutor! Rachel is truly one of the nicest people I have ever met.

Then there's Regan Bennett, a girl I knew from Beverly Hills Elementary. Regan and I have a complicated relationship, dating back to the second grade. I love Regan now, but there was a time when we were enemies. You'll understand why soon enough.

Other girls you'll meet include Kimberly Hachee, who is admittedly very shy. Kimberly is growing out of her shyness, thanks to the help of her best friend, Courtney Lee.

You'll meet Tammy Cleary, a very funny girl with a very funny story to tell about fitting in. (P.S. For those of you who don't know how to pronounce *my* first name, it rhymes with *Tammy*!)

You're also going to meet Monique White and Dana Shay, best friends who once hit some turbulence in their friendship because of a misunderstanding.

And last but not least, there's Brie Kaarup, another good friend from Beverly Hills. Brie came up with a great rule that has to do with friends who grow apart.

All these girls helped me so much in writing this book, and I owe them so much appreciation!

Okay, you're probably saying to yourself, "Let's get on with the rules!" But before I do, I want to say one more thing.

This book is about the beauty of friendship. One thing I've learned from experience, though, is that having a really great friendship takes a lot of work.

To have the *best* friendships possible, you have to commit yourself to making the effort. So before we go any further, I want you to read and sign the following contract.

I, _____ , do solemnly swear to give
your name here
1000% effort to my current and future friendships. I commit to making friends, and also doing whatever I

possibly can to make all my friendships fun, positive, and happy experiences. I know friendships can involve a lot of work, and I commit myself to these duties.

Signature _____ Date _____

Now that we have the legal formalities out of the way, let me introduce you to the wonderful, beautiful, exhilarating world of friendship!

part
one

always and forever cherish your true friends

I first met Rachel when she started going to Beverly Hills Elementary in the third grade. I mentioned earlier that Rachel's mother is a very famous movie star. (I still can't tell you who she is. But remember that movie . . . Just kidding—I can't tell!)

Rachel had it pretty rough at school. Since her mother is so famous, a lot of the other kids were jealous. I was never jealous of Rachel because that's not the way I am. And because I was never jealous, Rachel and I were able to become really good friends.

Last year Rachel decided to leave Beverly

Hills Elementary and travel with her mother, who is filming a new movie.

It's been a really wonderful experience for Rachel. She's seen a lot of different countries and cultures. Rachel doesn't get to see her friends a lot, but she gets to meet *new* ones in places like Australia, and Belgium, and even Japan!

Rachel and I have stayed in very close contact. I even had the chance to visit her in Hawaii while her mother was filming there! (More about that later!)

When I told Rachel I was writing this book, she was very excited. She said she had the perfect rule to start off with.

So, in the spirit of friendship, I want one of my closest pals to introduce the first rule of my book.

The following is an e-mail sent to me by Rachel, which sums up this very important rule.

Dear Camy,

My mother once told me that friendships are often based on location. I think what she means is that people usually hang out together when they live close to each other.

10

But a *true* friend is someone who is *always* with you. Even if you live a thousand miles away and can only e-mail or call on the phone, there's always one place you can find that friend. That place is in your heart. You'll know who that friend is because you'll think about them a lot.

I'm traveling with my mom now, so I don't have friends I see on a regular basis. But if I get lonely or sad, all I have to do is think about my true friends—like you, Camy—and I feel better.

I didn't realize how important my friends were to me. *Now* I know. Besides my mother, my friends are *the* most important thing in the world to me.

So if you ever have a bad day, or if anything bad ever comes into your life, think about your friends.

And if you ever have to move and are afraid you won't make any new friends, remember the true friends you left back home. Don't worry, though, you *will* make new friends!

"Always and forever cherish your true friends" means we can all find comfort in the beautiful gift of friendship.

Bye, Camy, and thanks for letting me share. I love and miss you!

Rachel

CAMY'S NOTE:

Rachel's rule really was the best one to start off with. It means you should never take your friends for granted. Each friend you have in your life really *is* a gift.

This is also a great rule because it's probably the easiest to follow! The only thing you have to do is love your friend with all your heart! How easy is *that*?

Before I go on to the next rule, I want to talk a little about friendship. Just *what* is it all about? See if you can guess what the best kind of friendship is. Pick the answer you think is most true:

1. The best kind of friendship is when you know every single detail about your friend's life and she knows every single detail about yours.

2. The best kind of friendship is when you care for, respect, and trust each other.

3. The best kind of friendship is when

your friend takes you to really cool parties and you meet *lots* of guys.

If you picked #3, then you are 1000% correct. What more can a friend do than help you get a boyfriend?!

NOOOOOOOOOOT!

Of course the correct answer is #2. The most you can ask for and the very least you should ask for, in any relationship is care, respect, and trust.

I have a little exercise for you. It will be painless, I promise! But it's very important.

I want you to stop reading this book for a minute and get a dictionary. Look up the words *care, respect,* and *trust.*

You probably think you already know the definitions. Sometimes, though, words like *care, respect,* and *trust* have more meaning then we might think!

After you look up the definitions, I want you to write in your journal, or on any piece of paper, your *own* definitions of the words. I'm going to refer to care, respect, and trust a lot in this book, so I *really* want you to know what they mean.

When you're done looking up the words, don't get distracted and start talking on the phone or something! You better finish reading my book! ☺

you'll make friends—
there's no need to force it

imagine for a moment that you're the new kid at school. You don't know anyone yet. How would you go about finding a new friend? Would you:

1. Wait for someone to introduce themselves to you?

2. Force your way into a group of girls and just start talking?

3. Smile at everyone you meet and say hi?

The problem with #1 is that unless you put yourself out there and let others know you're open to having a new friend, they might think you're stuck-up or shy.

But if you follow #2, you're just assuming a girl should be your friend because you want her to be. That's presumptuous. You should never be presumptuous. What does *presumptuous* mean?

According to my dictionary, *presumptuous* is when you think you know what others are thinking and feeling.

If I were presumptuous, I would just assume that Leonardo DiCaprio would be my boyfriend because I wanted him to be. I should first ask Leo if he *wants* to be my boyfriend, right? What if he already has a girlfriend?!!

If you're like me, you'll choose #3 and just keep saying hi until someone says hi back! If they do, you'll pretty much know they're open to having a new friend.

I would like to share a conversation I had with a friend of mine, Tammy, who goes to Peoria Middle School. Tammy learned that trying *too* hard to make friends can sometimes backfire.

CAMY: Thanks for sharing your story with

me. I know this must be pretty difficult for you.

TAMMY: Not really. I'm over it.

CAMY: At the time it must have been a really big deal.

TAMMY: I thought it was funny. My parents didn't, though.

CAMY: Why don't you tell me what happened?

TAMMY: Do you want the edited version or the long version?

CAMY: How long is the long version?

TAMMY: A couple of hours.

CAMY: How 'bout the edited version?

TAMMY: Okay. Well, I come from a small town in Alaska. My family moved to Illinois when I was ten. At the time I thought Illinois was going to be heaven on earth. Turns out it's just like Alaska, only not as cold.

I get here and I'm really clue-less. I thought the kids would be excited to meet me, you know? 'Cause Alaska is pretty interesting. I mean, I could tell you stories. . . .

CAMY: *(checks her watch)* Is this the edited version?

TAMMY: Sorry. So I get here and the other kids look at me like I'm weird. They walk around me whenever I pass through the halls. Must admit it was tough, but I decided not to be intimidated. I mean, once you've lived through an Alaskan winter . . .

So I go up to this girl who's standing all alone and I say, "Hi, my name is Tammy. Let's hang out at lunch, okay?" And she looks at me like . . . well, I don't know how she looked at me, but it was a weird look, kind of frightened, you know?

Lunchtime rolls around and I grab my food. And I see my new friend in the cafeteria. Turns out she's the most popular girl in school.

I sit next to her and her friends, and she goes, "What do you think you're doing?" I say, "I told you we were having lunch together."

She says, "I don't *think* so," just like in *Clueless*—only this was way before the movie! And then she goes, "I think the proper place for animals to be fed is *outside*."

Without even thinking, I pick up my casserole with this hand ... *(demonstrates for Camy)* and wipe it all over her face. Then I go, "Who's the animal *now*?"

Of course I got busted. As I'm led away by the principal, half the kids in the cafeteria start clapping because I slopped this girl with food. Which brings me to a question that I'm hoping you can answer for me.

CAMY: What's that?

TAMMY: Why is it that all the popular people seem to be the least liked?

CAMY: I've never really thought about it. Hey, Tam, let's talk about it after you wrap up this rule.

TAMMY: Sure, sure. So I came up with this rule because I realized you can't force yourself on people. You can't make just *anyone* be your friend. See, after this happened, I met a lot of girls just like me.

We have a lot of fun together, and I really feel like we're sisters, you know? This girl I wiped food on would never have been a good friend for me. Come on, she's a cheerleader now!

CAMY: Thanks for sharing, Tam.

CAMY'S NOTE:

It's important to mention that Tammy got detention for wiping food on the cheerleader.

I personally believe there are better ways to handle that sort of situation. Tammy could have *asked* the cheerleader if she wanted to have lunch. This is a free country, and no one is obligated to have lunch with anyone if they don't want to!

Tammy is a good example, though, of someone who takes the bull by the horns, as my dad likes to say. She isn't easily intimidated. She just needed to learn some manners! ☺

it's okay to make
the first move

in the previous rule, we talked about being new at school. Now let's pretend you've been going to the same school for a while. And there's this girl you would like to become friends with. But you guys haven't really said anything to each other before.

Someone's got to make the first move if you're going to be friends. Should it be you?

My friend Kimberly, who goes to Peoria Middle School, answered this very important question in the following letter.

Dear Camy,

I never thought in a thousand years Courtney and I would be friends. I'm pretty shy. Courtney, though, is real outgoing and has tons of friends.

Courtney's parents became friends with my parents. They all started playing cards together every Wednesday night at our house, and Courtney would come over with them.

She usually hung out with my two brothers and played basketball. I just read or did homework in my room. I could hear them playing out back, and it made me jealous.

To be honest, I was afraid to go down there and join them. My brothers are really evil and like to torture me. Besides, I was afraid Courtney wouldn't like me. We knew each other and stuff, but we weren't, like, friends.

It really bothered me that I was being so shy. It was like I was hiding out in my room!

Finally I realized I was being unfair to myself. I wasn't giving Courtney a chance to know me. "Maybe she would like me," I reminded myself.

Even though I was frightened, I finally

just did it. I went downstairs and told them I wanted to play basketball.

Courtney was totally cool about it. She said, "It's about time. These creeps can't play worth anything!"

My brothers started the name-calling, trying to embarrass me. Courtney stood up for me. She said she wouldn't play basketball with them unless they stopped.

Courtney and I played on the same team. I was surprised to find out I'm a pretty good basketball player. Together, Courtney and I never lost a game to my brothers! They hated it!

Courtney and I later started hanging out in my room, just talking and stuff. It was so funny. Courtney said she thought I didn't want to be her friend because I never came out of my room! Isn't that strange? I was dying to be her friend, and here she thought I didn't want to!

Anyway, Courtney and I found out we had a lot in common. It only took a few weeks before we realized we had become best friends!

I'm lucky because Courtney and I were thrown together. Had it not been for our *parents' weekly card games, we never would have had a chance to really get to know each other. That makes me realize there are probably tons of girls out there who aren't friends but should be.*

At school it's hard for girls to get to know shy people like me. We usually bury our heads in books or just keep quiet.

But I've learned it's a two-way street to starting a friendship.

Shy girls and outgoing girls (and we all know who we are!) should try this: Next time you see each other, just smile and say hi.

It might take a few times before anything happens. But if you keep doing it, pretty soon you're going to say something else besides hi.

And who knows—maybe you'll find yourself talking to a girl who will soon be your new best friend!

CAMY'S NOTE:

Kimberly admitted she was afraid of putting herself out there and becoming friends with

Courtney. She also made a great point: Friendships are a two-way street.

What that really means is that for two people to become friends, they both have to (1) *try* to become friends, and (2) *want* to become friends.

So what if you try to become a girl's friend and she doesn't want to be your friend? That leads me to my next rule:

4

everyone gets rejected once in a while

how would you react if you said hi to a girl you wanted to become friends with and she didn't say anything back? Would you:

1. Let this rejection hurt your feelings and ruin your day?

2. Blow the rejection off and say, "What's *her* problem"?

If you picked #2, you are a strong, confident person. Because if you introduce yourself to a girl and she doesn't respond, there's nothing wrong with *you*. In fact, I would say there's something wrong with *her*.

Either she's in a bad mood; or she's not friendly; or she's mean to girls she doesn't know. But this rejection is not your fault, so you should *not* take it personally.

I know it's probably the single most embarrassing thing we can experience when we say hi to someone and they don't say hi back.

But if you understand this rule that everyone gets rejected once in a while—you're going to be able to say hi without fear.

I had to remember this rule a few months back when my mom and I went to California for a visit.

There I was, in the Beverly Center, the best mall in the world. I was having a great time because I had two hundred dollars to buy anything I wanted. (I had been saving for *months!*) I bought two pairs of shoes and a belt, and then I treated my mom to lunch.

After lunch we headed to the car. I saw two girls I thought I recognized, my friends Pam and Lisa. So I ran over to them. When I got closer I realized it wasn't Pam and Lisa at all, but two girls I had never seen before.

The girls noticed me. I thought it would be rude to walk away without an explanation, so I went over and introduced myself.

27

The girls didn't say a word. They just looked me up and down—at my shoes, my clothes, my hair.

Then they turned to each other, started giggling, and walked away!

I stood there speechless. What was wrong? Did I have toilet paper hanging from my shoe? Was I wearing a "Kick Me, I'm Stupid" sticker on my shirt?

I ran over to a mirror and checked my clothes. *Everything* was fine. I couldn't figure out why they'd laughed at me. Then I realized the awful truth. They were mean.

After a few seconds of feeling embarrassed, I just let it go. I wasn't going to let *them* ruin my great shopping day.

Now that I'm not afraid to say hi, I meet *lots* of people. And a lot of those people have become very good friends of mine.

As for the girls who *don't* want to be my friend: their loss!

conversations are easy—
don't be afraid of them

Once you meet a person, you're on the road to making a new friend.

But after you get past that initial meeting, the next step is to *talk* to this person. And for some girls, this is a very difficult thing to do.

I must admit, since my nickname is Chatterbox Baker, I talk. A *lot*. And I find it difficult to understand why some girls have a hard time talking to other people. Fortunately I have an older sister who has been able to fill me in.

My sister, Sara, is naturally shy. She used to be terrified of speaking to people she just met. Sara's growing out of her shyness, and you

29

probably will too. Talking with people you don't know is really easy. It just takes practice.

I'm not insisting you talk. Talking or not talking is your choice. But this is a book about friendship and I'm assuming you're reading it as a way to make more friends. After all, the only way to get to *know* someone is to talk with them!

To make conversation easier for you, I've come up with a few tips.

Pretend for a moment you're at a school dance. And you're new to the school. Fortunately you've made a friend who introduces you to a group of girls.

Tip #1: Stand tall and feel confident. *Anyone* can feel confident. Confidence is a state of mind we can all choose to have. Confidence will be your secret weapon!

Tip #2: As you're introduced to the girls and say hello, look each of them in the eye. Eye contact reinforces to the girls that you're very confident.

After you're introduced, the girls will probably want to know a little something about you. They may ask where you are from, what your old school was like, etc.

Tip #3: When asked a question, always be open and honest with your answers. Don't try to tell the girls what you *think* they want to hear. That will make you feel pressured. You'll never really know if you're saying the right thing.

You know what the right thing to say is? The truth. Try to be direct and honest and real. If you're a straight-A student, tell the girls you're really into school and what your favorite subject is.

Or if you're into sports, tell them. Maybe someone in the group plays the same sport. This could really open up the conversation!

Once the girls are done asking you questions, they'll probably start talking about other things.

Maybe they'll talk about a particular boy they all find cute. You, obviously, don't know the boy.

Tip #4: To stay involved in the conversation, ask a question. Ask them which boy they're talking about. What's his name? Has anyone in the group ever gone out with him?

Tip #5: Don't feel like you're asking a stupid question. No question is stupid. If you think,

"Gosh, was that a stupid question!" then you might feel too embarrassed to ask any more.

Tip #6: If there's a lull in the conversation (a lull is when the conversation stops and no one talks for a minute), ask the girls if they've seen the new Will Smith movie. Or ask if anyone has heard the new CD of a group you think *rocks*. Chances are someone in the group has seen the movie or heard the CD. This could get the conversation going.

Tip #7: Another great thing to do is talk one-on-one with a girl in the group. It's perfectly acceptable for two girls to break away from the group and start talking between themselves. It will probably be easier for you to talk with just one girl, instead of several at a time.

Tip #8: Once you start talking to the girl, pay her a compliment. Tell her you like her sweater (if you really do).

Tip #9: Or ask her about herself. Maybe she'll tell you something that triggers a response. For instance, maybe she'll say she has her own horse. If you *love* horses, this could really get your conversation going!

Even if you follow all of the above tips and

you still feel like the other girls are not accepting you into their group, that's okay! It's not *your* fault.

Some girls could just be mean; or they could be difficult to get to know; or maybe they feel threatened by you because you're new. Chances are this won't happen. But if it does, if you're ever made to feel uncomfortable, then you should follow this last tip.

Tip #10: Excuse yourself and go get a soda. Walk outside and get some fresh air. Who knows? Maybe you'll come across another girl standing alone. You can say hi. If she says hi back, then use the above tips and start talking with *her*!

As Kimberly said earlier, if you make the first move, you might end up talking to a girl who could someday become your new best friend!

And if you follow these few simple tips, you'll soon be talking to anyone about anything without fear!

learn how to listen

I've said before that I love to talk. Lord knows, I love to talk! But do you want to know something funny? It has taken me many years to learn how to *listen*.

If you're like me, you think everything you have to say is very important. And it probably is. But you have to remember that what your friends have to say is *just* as important.

Sadly, I must admit I *never* used to listen! But then a friend from Beverly Hills threatened to quit speaking with me unless I paid attention to what *she* was saying! I really valued that friendship, so I started to listen *very* quickly!

Listening seems like it's pretty easy, right?

Well, the thing I've learned is that listening is a very active process. To be a good listener, you first need to pay attention to what's being said.

When others are talking, you should never just pretend to hear what they say, then launch right back into what you want to talk about.

Think about it. How do you feel if you're talking to a friend and you can tell she isn't paying attention to you? You feel insulted, right? It's like she doesn't even care what you have to say! Well, if you don't listen to her, she'll be insulted too!

Another great way to show you're a really good listener is to ask questions. When you ask a question about something a person is talking about, you show that you're paying attention.

Listening to your friend—*really* listening to her—is one of the most important ingredients of a very successful friendship. Because when you're listening to your friend, you're respecting what she has to say.

And if you respect what your friend has to say, chances are she's going to respect *you*! ☺

try to have a varied group of friends

friends come in all different shapes, colors, and styles. Like a really cool shoe collection!

Let's face it, though. We tend to choose friends who are similar to us in some way. Either they live in our neighborhood, or look like us, or dress like us, or go to the same church as us. It's perfectly natural to want to find a friend you have something in common with.

For instance, let's take a look at my best friend, Jackie, and me.

Jackie's dad is a construction worker; my dad is an electrician. Jackie's mom works at a grocery store; my mom goes to junior college.

36

Jackie's brother, Louis, is twenty, and he goes to the same school as my mom. My sister, Sara, is nineteen, and she goes to the University of Illinois.

Jackie and I live in similar houses and go to the same church (when we can't get out of it). We really have a lot in common!

But I came up with this rule to remind you that it's okay to develop a friendship with someone who doesn't look, act, or dress anything like you.

Let me give you an example. At first a lot of girls at Beverly Hills Elementary weren't interested in becoming my friend because they knew I came from a middle-class background.

But Rachel didn't care about my family's income. She was more interested in finding out who I was as a person. And because of this, I think Rachel and I will be FF (Friends Forever).

But it wasn't always easy for Rachel and me to be friends. When we went shopping, Rachel always had enough money to buy whatever she wanted. It was hard for me not to be able to shop as much as she could shop. I think Rachel figured this out, because she didn't want to hang out at the mall so much anymore.

On the flip side, it was hard at first for Rachel to see my mom and dad together and happy, because her parents got divorced when she was five. In fact, *most* of the kids in Beverly Hills had divorced parents. But because she had me as a friend, Rachel was always included in my family's activities. My mom started calling Rachel her third daughter. Rachel loved it and felt less lonely when her mother was away filming a movie.

I had another great experience in Beverly Hills that helped me come up with this rule: I became better friends with a girl who had a different religion than me.

In the fourth grade, I sent out tons of Christmas cards to the girls in my class. One of the girls, Brooke, came back to school after the holiday break and said thanks for the card. But she also reminded me that she's Jewish and celebrates Hanukkah, not Christmas.

I was embarrassed because I totally forgot. Also I wasn't even really sure what Hanukkah was all about. Brooke was totally cool about it. She spent time telling me what the holidays were like for her. After that experience we became a lot closer, and I now know more about the Jewish religion!

And then there are the boys. A lot of girls think boys are there to date and that's it. But since I don't have a boyfriend yet (I'm *still* waiting, girls, still waiting), I have instead become really good friends with some totally cool guys.

Having a friend who's a boy is really good experience. I'm sure it will come in handy when I actually start dating one. Now I know a lot about how boys think! ☺

You can become friends with adults, too. For instance, Jackie volunteers every other Sunday at the local senior citizens' home. Jackie has developed a really great friendship with Marika, a woman who is ninety-five years old! Marika tells Jackie all these great stories about her very long life. Marika had emigrated from a country in Europe, and now Jackie wants to take a trip to Marika's home country when she gets old enough to travel on her own.

So my point is, *anyone* can be your friend. There are tons of nice people out there who don't dress, act, or look anything like you. And just because they don't look like you on the surface doesn't mean they aren't exactly like you on the inside. So take a chance. Have a varied groups of friends.

Because you'll probably learn a *lot* of great things that you otherwise wouldn't get to know! ☺

it's okay not to have a best friend

Some girls have many best friends; other girls don't have any. If you don't have a best friend right now, it doesn't mean there's anything wrong with you.

When we decide to have a best friend, all it means is that we've chosen a particular friend to be really close with. That's it. No one hands out certificates that say you and your pal are now best friends. It's just a choice girls make.

You are a unique and special person, and it's important to find the friendships that fit you best. It's not always easy to find people you

41

have a lot in common with. It takes time, and even a little bit of luck.

You could go your *whole* school year and not find a special friend you feel really close to. Then BOOM, a new girl arrives and you have a lot in common.

You and this girl become friends, you spend more time together, and then you realize you have a best friend. *Voilà!*

When I first moved to Peoria, I had friends, but I didn't have a best friend. And I was okay with that. I mean, when I'd hear a girl talk about her best friend, it left me feeling a little sad.

But instead of dwelling on it, I put all my efforts into my hobbies and my schoolwork. I got so much stuff done. I've never been more productive in my life!

Then I met Jackie in the library. We happened to be looking for the same book for a paper we were writing on the Civil War.

Jackie and I went for the book at the same time. We almost started to fight over it, but the librarian suggested we share it. It was one of those suggestions that make so much sense— and probably changed our lives. By doing our research together, we planted the seed for a really great friendship!

Anyway, if you don't have a best friend right now, don't worry. If you want one, you'll find one. Just be patient. It happens *all* the time. And it will probably happen when you least expect it!

a bet in maui

it all started with a phone call.

Rachel, one of my dear friends from Beverly Hills Elementary, called me from the set of her mother's movie in Hawaii.

Rachel had been traveling with her mother from country to country. When the movie started filming in Hawaii, Rachel begged her mother to let a friend visit. Her mother agreed. Rachel invited *me*!

Of course my parents said no when I asked permission. They always say no to stuff like that. They said we couldn't afford it.

I was so mad, I didn't talk to my parents for

a week. That was really hard. I kept forgetting I was mad at them!

Was I surprised when Rachel called back and said her mother offered to pay for my trip!

My parents still didn't think it was a good idea. I begged. I pleaded. I cajoled and threatened and hissed and barked and did everything I could to make my parents say yes.

"It's spring break!" I reminded them. "I'll never have a chance like this again!!! Please!!!"

My parents finally said yes. You'd think I'd asked to get married or something!

But there I was, on a plane to Maui. I went first class! Go, Camy, go!

Seeing Rachel was the bomb. She looked great. She was tan and wore a really cool Hawaiian dress with a flower design.

Rachel's mom was wonderful! Every free moment she had from the movie, she took us sight-seeing.

We even rented a helicopter and flew over all the Hawaiian Islands. It was so dreamy, watching the sun set against the majestic blue water. I thought I was in heaven . . . !

Until Regan arrived.

What were the chances? The world is a pretty big place. Why did Regan and her father *have* to vacation in Maui?!

Regan was my one and only enemy at Beverly Hills Elementary. We had never gotten along, ever since the second grade. She was the most controlling person I had ever met. A lot of the other girls at school worshipped her. Regan is very pretty and she dresses well, but she was not a very nice person.

Regan loved to make fun of me. She couldn't stand the fact that I was a writer.

"Camy, it's great how modest you are about your books," she said. "I guess it's because you come from such a modest family."

I tried to be Regan's friend, I really did. But she never accepted me. She looked down on me because my dad was "just an electrician," in her words.

When Rachel and I discovered Regan was staying at our hotel, we avoided her like the plague. But it was no use.

One day down by the pool, Rachel and I were in the middle of a conversation about a concert we were going to. Suddenly Regan appeared out of nowhere and sat down in a lawn chair beside us.

Rachel and I both looked at each other and rolled our eyes. Rachel and Regan never got along, even though they both come from wealthy parents who are divorced. On the surface Regan and Rachel seemed a *lot* alike. Deep down they were total opposites!

Rachel and I excused ourselves and went down to the beach. Fortunately Regan didn't tag along.

Later that night Rachel and her mother and I were eating dinner in the hotel's restaurant. And guess who showed up? Regan and her father. And Rachel's mother invited them to eat with us!

You'd better sit down for this next part.

RACHEL'S MOM AND REGAN'S DAD WERE ATTRACTED TO EACH OTHER!!!! Can you believe it? During dessert Regan's father asked Rachel's mother on a *date*! And she accepted!

Oh, it was the worst for Rachel. After dinner she begged, pleaded, cajoled, threatened, barked, and demanded that her mother not see

Regan's father. But Rachel's mother explained how difficult it is to meet people who like her for *her*, not because she's a movie star.

And Regan's father *is* a nice guy. How he spawned that *thing* he has for a daughter is beyond me.

Anyway, it was weird. There was a very horribly real potential that Rachel and Regan could one day be stepsisters!!!!

The next day Rachel and I were watching television. There was a knock on our hotel room door. I opened the door, and of course it was Regan. She barged into our room and plopped herself on Rachel's bed.

Rachel and I stared at each other in exasperation. Who did this girl think she was? She didn't say two words to us, but stormed into our room without being invited!

Regan picked up the remote and turned on *Beavis and Butt-head*! That was the final straw. I had finally *had* it. Regan was ruining our vacation!

I impulsively said, "Regan, I'll make a bet with you."

"What kind of bet?" she said. "It certainly couldn't be for money."

Oooooooh, how she irritated me! I took a deep breath and calmed myself. "You know that BoyzLife concert is coming up, right?" I asked.

BoyzLife is one of my favorite boy groups. Rachel's mom got us tickets to the concert. Unfortunately she got Regan a ticket as well.

"Yeah? So what about BoyzLife?" Regan asked.

"I bet I can kiss the lead singer of BoyzLife before you can." This was a devious bet. I knew Regan's weakness was her competitive streak when it came to boys.

"It'll be a cold day in hell before you kiss a boy before me."

"So you want to bet or what?" I asked, irritated by her language.

"What do I win?"

"Well, *if* you win—and that's a big *if*—then I'll get a T-shirt made that says, 'Regan is the prettiest, smartest, most fabulous girl in the whole world.' And I'll wear it for the rest of the time we're in Maui."

"Oh boy," I thought, "I better win." We had another week left and I *really* didn't want to wear that T-shirt.

"You'll wear it twenty-four/seven, right?"

"Ugh, right," I added nervously.

Regan thought about it for a second. I could see a light shining in her eyes. She wanted nothing more than to see me wear that T-shirt. *What* had I gotten myself into?

"And—which I doubt will happen—if I *lose*?" she asked, like she never believed in a thousand years it was possible.

"Then . . ." I hesitated, thinking.

Rachel was looking at me eagerly. I hadn't planned to make this bet. But now I had to come up with something good. "Then, ugh— Rachel and I will not have to be around you for the rest of our trip. Deal?"

For a moment I caught something in Regan's eyes. And what it looked like—no, it couldn't be—but it kind of looked like . . . *sadness*. Had I hurt her feelings?

Couldn't Regan tell Rachel and I couldn't stand her? If only she were nicer, maybe we could all get along. But she was so *mean*!

As soon as I saw the look, it was gone. Regan said, "You think I like hanging around with you irritants? I might just lose that bet so I don't have to see your faces anymore." She stuck out her hand, and I shook it.

Rachel clapped loudly and said, "Right on!"

Regan stood up, took one last look at us, then marched out of the room and slammed the door.

As soon as Regan was gone, Rachel jumped up excitedly. "Camy, you've got to win that bet," she said. "You've just got to!"

"Yeah," I said weakly. But staring at that closed door, why did I feel like I had just done something really awful?

it's *okay* to fight

fights between friends are perfectly natural. They happen all the time. Most of the time friends remain friends even after fights. Fights are just a way of resolving problems we might not realize are affecting the friendship.

It just so happens that my best friend, Jackie, came up with this rule. It's weird, though— Jackie and I had the biggest fight we've ever had *because* of this rule!

Before I go into my blowout with Jackie, I have to set the situation up a bit.

When I first started writing this book, Jackie was really, really excited about coming up with a rule for me. After she came up with a cool rule, I told her I would interview her so she could explain it to you, the readers.

But I think I hurt her feelings. I really didn't like any of the rules she suggested. In my defense, I'm kind of picky about what I put in my book and I simply couldn't use any of the rules Jackie brought me.

Then Jackie finally came up with this rule. Perfect, I thought!

I set up an appointment to interview her. Jackie was *way* irritated about that. She said, "You need an appointment to interview your *best* friend?!"

What Jackie didn't take into account is that I am very serious about my writing, *very* professional. It takes time to think up questions, write them out, get plenty of tape and batteries for my recorder. It's, like, *work*. But she didn't get it.

So the day of the interview finally arrived. When Jackie came over to my house, I could already tell she was in a bad mood. And when Jackie's in a bad mood—LOOK OUT! She gets really sensitive about *everything*.

After having a Diet Pepsi, we finally sat down at the kitchen table for the interview. I turned on the tape recorder.

This is what happened.

CAMY: Thanks for doing this interview, Jacko!!!!

JACKIE: Don't call me Jacko again or I'm going to *hurt* you.

CAMY: *(laughs)* Very funny. Seriously, Jacko, why don't you tell everyone about your rule.

JACKIE: I'm serious, Camy. *Don't* call me Jacko! That's what they call Michael Jackson in England, and he truly freaks me out!

CAMY: *(perplexed)* You're kidding, right? I call you Jacko all the time!

JACKIE: Yeah, but when we're alone. Or maybe when Katy and Sheila are around. I don't want the girls reading your book to know about my stupid nickname. Is this thing recording? *(taps the tape recorder)* Can we start over?

CAMY: Yeah, I guess. I can just edit the

	other stuff out—no big deal. So let's just start again. Ready?
JACKIE:	Yeah.
CAMY:	Okay. So *Jacqueline,* why don't you tell me about—
JACKIE:	*(screams) What* are you *doing*?!?
CAMY:	*(confused)* What . . . ?
JACKIE:	My name's *Jackie*! Not Jacko, and not Jacqueline! *What* is your problem today?!
CAMY:	*My* problem? What is *your* problem?! If you're going to be this way, I'm not interviewing you!
JACKIE:	Great. I knew it! You didn't want me in your book *anyway*!
CAMY:	*What* are you talking about?! Of course I want you in my book!
JACKIE:	Then why did I have to beg you?!
CAMY:	You didn't! I told you I would interview you after you came up with a good rule.
JACKIE:	And why did you put that girl Rachel first?! Explain *that*!
CAMY:	She had the best rule to start off with! I didn't have a place for you until you came up with this rule.

JACKIE: Oh, so now it's my fault?! You think I'm too stupid to come up with a rule?! All these rules are stupid anyway! You know what *your* problem is? *You're* just afraid I might have something funny or interesting to say and make you look bad!

CAMY: I *wish* you had something funny or interesting to say, because you're really starting to make me mad!

JACKIE: I don't want to be in your stupid book anyway! *(Jackie knocks the tape recorder off the table. Recording ends.)*

The tragic interview was over. Jackie stormed out of the room.

but *don't* fight over boys

before I finish telling you how things turned out with Jackie, I want to put this rule out there because I think it's very, very important.

As I said before, fights between friends are natural and normal. But there's one thing you should *never* fight over: boys!

Chances are, a friendship is going to last longer than a relationship with a boy. Sure, some friendships only last a few months, though most last a year or maybe two—heck, maybe for the rest of your life.

But when it comes to going out with a boy?!

I'm sorry, if boy-girl relationships were milk cartons, we'd have to put expiration dates on them because they'd spoil fast!

Okay, okay, you're probably saying to yourself, "Camy's a little bitter because she hasn't had a real boyfriend yet." Maybe. *Maybe.*

Really, though. How many of your friends who have boyfriends stay with them more than a few weeks—a few months at the most? Count them up.

If I'm wrong here, then send me a letter and maybe I'll change my opinion on the matter. From what I've seen, though, most couples our age don't stay together for more than a few weeks.

The rule basically means you should never let a boy come between you and a friend for *any* reason. For instance, Jackie once had a boyfriend who didn't like me. He called me a snob because I once went to Beverly Hills Elementary.

I overheard him telling a friend what he thought about me. Did I tell Jackie? No. I didn't want her to think I was trying to break them up.

Instead I waited. Sure enough, Jackie found

out what a slime this boy was. I didn't have to lift a finger, they broke up, and Jackie and I remained the best of friends! No boy was going to come between *us*.

Doesn't stop us from fighting, though!

Speaking of fights, I'm sure you're dying to hear how everything turned out! Well, read on. Our huge fight helped me come up with the next rule:

take some time to cool down

Sometimes fights happen over really small things.

Say a friend forgets your birthday. Or a friend borrows something and never returns it. Or a friend uses your computer and accidentally deletes a really important file—like the picture of Brad Pitt you downloaded off the Internet! J.k. (Just kidding.)

None of these things is a very big deal, and a simple apology from your friend can fix them.

But that fight I had with Jackie—whoa, *something* else was going on *there*. She had some major issues to uncover because she verbally and almost physically assaulted me for no reason!

Two hours after the fight, Jackie sent me an e-mail apologizing for breaking my tape recorder and offering to buy me a new one. I sent her an e-mail accepting her apology but said we needed some time apart.

Jackie sent me an e-mail back asking why I thought we needed some time apart, and how long I thought I needed.

I sent Jackie an e-mail saying I thought we needed time apart because she needs time to think about why she freaked out like that. And I said I would probably need about a week.

Jackie sent back an e-mail saying okay.

It was a *long* week. It's very difficult not to speak to someone when (1) she rides your bus, (2) she lives in your neighborhood, (3) she has all the same classes you have, and (4) she shares the same friends.

The rumors were rampant! The whole school was freaking out because Jackie and I weren't talking to each other.

The days finally passed. I still hadn't gotten any closer to the truth about why she'd wigged out like that. But I *did* miss her.

It was hard at school not to run up and hug her and say, "I'm sorry. Let's not ever fight again!" But I knew there was something deep down in Jackie that caused her to act the way she did.

If I just forgave her without giving *her* time to think about what happened, I knew the same thing might happen all over again.

When the week was over, Jackie and I sat down in my kitchen to talk. Before I could say anything, Jackie blurted out:

"The conclusion I've come to this week is that I'm jealous of your writing. It's not something I'm normally included in. And I just got the feeling you didn't want me to be in the book.

"I know I overreacted," she continued. "I guess I was too sensitive. But it hurt me that it took you so long to finally interview me. So when you *finally* did, I guess I was nervous and upset."

I took a second to think about what Jackie had just said. It made total sense. Jackie was feeling hurt and a little jealous because of my writing. She felt like I was excluding her. It made her feel insecure.

I told her, "You *know* you're my best friend in the world! I share the things I write with you before *anybody*! Whenever I write something I'm excited about, who do I call first? You! When I print out something I've written, who's the first person to see it? You."

"It's true. All of it. But I guess I'm also jealous because your writing isn't something we do together," she said.

"I guess *that's* how I felt when you dated the Boy Who Shall Remain Nameless," I countered.

"Did you have to bring up *that* troll?" Jackie said, crinkling her nose. Then she asked, "You were jealous?"

"A little," I admitted. "I was happy for you, definitely. But I was worried our friendship would change because of him."

"Never! Not *him,*" she said. "Oh, Camy, let's not fight! I mean, we can fight, but let's not go a week without talking. It was unbearable, and *everyone* was talking about it! Next time let's just make up as soon as we can, okay?"

"Jackie, it was hard for me too, not talking. But do you really think we would have figured all this out if we didn't take that week off? Sometimes it's too easy just apologizing. Sometimes it takes time to figure things out."

"Yeah, I guess. Well, I'll try not to get all

weird about things. I'll try to be a little more understanding."

"Me too. And I'll never call you Jacko in an interview again!" I said.

"Oh, I have a surprise for you, Camy."

As I love surprises, I was very excited. "You got me a present?!"

"Kind of."

Jackie pulled a band-new tape recorder out of her bag. She had bought it for me to replace the one she had broken. It was ten times better than the old one! It was so cool! It was smaller and it had a *lot* more features.

"Jackie, this *rocks*! Let's get into fights more often!" Jackie and I looked at each other at the same time. "Just kidding!" we said in unison. Then we hugged.

Our biggest fight ever was *officially* over.

12

show your friend you care

at the root of any good friendship is caring. I know I've said this before, but caring really is the essential ingredient of a good relationship! Caring brings you closer to your friend, making your relationship better.

How do you know if you're a caring person? And how do you know if someone cares for you?

Sometimes caring is hard to see. When you care for someone, it's usually a silent thing you hold in your heart.

One way to show that you really care about your friend is to do something nice for her, *for no reason at all!*

Send her a card, even if there's no special occasion. Or be creative and *make* a card on a computer! I make cards for my friends all the time!

Jackie did something for me the other night that was so cool! Jackie loves to cook. She's been helping her mom in the kitchen for years, and she's really good. (I, for one, am *not* a good cook! I'm learning, though.)

Anyway, Jackie invited me over to her house and surprised me with a really great dinner! She made chicken breasts, rolled up and pinned with toothpicks. Inside the chicken was my favorite—stuffing! It was the *bomb*!

After dinner I asked Jackie what the occasion was. And you know what she told me? She goes, "Just because."

It made me feel really wonderful about our relationship. It reminded me she *really* does care about me.

Besides saying thank you, about the easiest thing you can do during your day is a random act of kindness. Send your friend a card, make her a special lunch or dinner, bake her cookies, help with her homework, or simply give her a hug.

All just to show you care! It will mean a lot to your friend. But the best thing is, it will make you feel really good about *yourself*!

13

don't push too hard

Imagine this: Your best friend comes to school and she looks really upset. She's been crying and barely speaks to you.

You know something's up and ask if she's okay. She says, "I'm fine," and then rushes away. What do you do? Do you:

1. Run after her and scream until she breaks down and tells you what's wrong?

2. Watch her rush away and wonder what it is *you* did wrong?

3. Realize something really bad has happened and decide to give her some space?

If you picked #3, then you are a really awesome friend. You understand something is upsetting your friend, but you're going to give her time to tell you about it.

It hurts when a friend is in pain and she won't let you in to help her. If this ever happens to you, the most important thing to remember is that your friend isn't *rejecting* you. Your friend just isn't ready to talk about the thing that is hurting her.

I want to share with you a conversation between my friends Dana and Monique that sums up this rule.

Dana and Monique go to my school, Peoria Middle School, and have been best friends since the second grade. Dana is a wild tomboy who plays softball. Monique is a quiet, sensitive musician. She's brilliant at the piano.

One day their friendship was perfect. Then suddenly, overnight, their friendship was in jeopardy because Monique was shutting Dana out, making Dana feel like she had done something wrong.

I'll let them explain why, in this interview I did with them.

CAMY: I'm glad you guys were able to patch everything up. For the record, you're best friends again.

DANA: Totally. It was real rocky there for a few weeks, though. I didn't understand what was happening.

CAMY: Monique, do you want to start?

MONIQUE: Well, um—really, this whole thing started *way* before the big fight with Dana. There was something going on at home that Dana didn't even know about. I never told her. I didn't want to believe it myself.

CAMY: *(to Dana)* You had no idea Monique was having trouble at home?

DANA: *None.* I mean, I spend a lot of time at Monique's, and if there had been a problem, it seems like I would have known something. But *nada.*

MONIQUE: There was a lot of denial going on around my house. Looking back at how my parents handled the situation, it makes me very mad at them.

CAMY: *(to Monique)* Do you mind telling me what was going on?

MONIQUE: *(quiet for a moment)* One day I came home and my father had moved out. My parents were getting a divorce. They didn't give me *any* warning! I mean, I knew they fought and stuff, but they always assured me that it was perfectly normal and I shouldn't worry. So I didn't worry.

But then it happened. My dad was gone. I completely shut down, blanked everything out.

DANA: All I knew was that one day at school she was fine, and the next day at school she was like a zombie. I knew right away something was wrong. But she *totally* avoided me. I felt maybe *I* had done something wrong. When I tried talking to her about it, she said everything

71

was fine and *I* was the one with the problem. That made me so mad! Instead of staying calm, I went off! I guess I was trying to force her to tell me what was going on. She started crying right there in front of everyone.

MONIQUE: It was pretty embarrassing. I missed the next couple of days of school. I just couldn't face anyone.

DANA: I was *really* confused. Everyone at school asked me what I did, and I was, like, I don't *know*. I was numb and sad. I left a message on Monique's machine and was, like, sobbing. I begged her to call me. I said I was sorry about a thousand times.

CAMY: *(to Monique)* Did you call her back?

MONIQUE: *(nods)* I called Dana and admitted something really bad had happened, but it wasn't about her. I still couldn't tell her about the divorce, though. It took me a few days.

DANA: After she called, I felt better. I figured her parents must have split up, though.

When Monique finally came back to school, I didn't push her to talk. I decided to let her tell me when she was ready.

I'd learned my lesson. Friends talk about things when they're ready. And my pushing her to talk made it pretty awful for both of us.

CAMY: You learned from your mistake?

DANA: Definitely!

CAMY'S NOTE:

How we deal with a bad situation is different for everybody. Some girls like to talk about a problem with their friends immediately after it happens.

Others, like Monique, need time to let the situation become more real to them. Monique was in pain. Talking about it too soon was not the best thing for her.

You should *always* be there for a friend when she needs you. Sometimes, though, she just won't let you in.

Don't push. Instead, let her know that when she's ready to talk, you're ready to listen. She'll appreciate it. She *really* will.

By the way, are you curious about the *bet*? I bet you are!

a bet in maui—part 2

the day of the concert was just like any other day. Rachel and I awoke in our own private suite to a glorious sunrise. Our hotel room overlooked the ocean, and I could hear seagulls rustling around looking for food out on the beach.

Rachel's mom had to work all day, so our chaperone came into the room bright and early to take us down to breakfast.

After breakfast Rachel and I headed to the beach and lay out—wearing sunscreen, of course.

Rachel questioned me nonstop, wondering

how I was going to win the bet. What I didn't tell her was the truth. I had *no* idea.

Besides, I wasn't even sure I *wanted* to win the bet. When I voiced this to Rachel, she asked me if I wanted to wear that T-shirt praising Regan.

I started to formulate a plan, like, *yesterday*!

The concert was at an auditorium with a view of the ocean. We arrived in a limousine paid for by Rachel's mother. It was funny watching all the other kids staring at us enviously as we arrived.

Regan stepped out of the limousine first, totally loving the attention. She was wearing a really low-cut red dress that my parents wouldn't let me be caught dead in. In fact, if they caught me in that dress, they might *kill* me!

Every single guy gawked at Regan. I really hate that. Guys look so stupid when their eyes bulge like that. They look like guppies. I, for one, am not attracted to guppies.

Rachel got out of the limousine next. She was wearing a flower-print dress, nice but nothing revealing.

I got out last. I was wearing a simple outfit:

white T-shirt, Levi's, way-cool blue clogs, and a thrift store jacket. Of course I looked *FIERCE,* but I knew the bet wouldn't be won on looks. No, I was going to win this bet with my smarts.

The concert *rocked.*

Rachel, Regan, and I had seats in the front row, though we didn't sit for a minute. The girls behind us kept pushing against us, trying to get closer to the stage. They were screaming like banshees, and it was hard to hear the music.

As the concert was nearing the end, the girls screamed louder and louder. Some were crying! I was, like, get a *life.* But I had to admit the guys in BoyzLife *were* adorable.

As the concert ended, the crazy girls behind us stormed the stage. Bodyguards rushed forward and tried to push the girls back.

Regan saw her cue. She pushed her way through the crowd toward the lead singer up on the stage.

I didn't waste a minute. I knew it would be foolish to go the same route as the other girls. I would never make it to the lead singer in time. Instead I pushed my way to the side of the stage, where I saw a thick rope hanging from a rafter.

It was tough getting through the crowd. Everyone was screaming and pushing. It was chaos!

Over the noise I heard Rachel screaming, "Go, Camy! Go!"

I felt light, like I was running on air. Time seemed to stop. All I could think about was getting to that rope!

I climbed to the top of a really big speaker at the edge of the stage. I reached for the rope, just barely able to grab it. Luckily I had worn my three-inch-high clogs!

I looked out over the crowd. The guards had stopped the mass of screaming girls from rushing onto the stage. I spotted Regan in her shiny red dress. She and the other girls were packed together so tightly they looked like cattle. Boyz-Life was still on the stage, looking confused.

I looked at the lead singer of BoyzLife. I think he looked up at me. I aimed.

Before I knew it, my feet were gliding through the air. I swung across the stage, holding on to the rope like Tarzan. It seemed like I swung forever, but it was probably only about three seconds.

I closed my eyes. I let go of the rope. When I

opened my eyes, I was in the arms of the lead singer. "Hi," I said nervously. Then I kissed his cheek.

I don't remember much after that. I think he said hi back and smiled. The one thing I do remember is that he smelled like he had just eaten a salami sandwich. Am I glad I didn't try to kiss him on the lips! He set me down, and then he and the rest of the group ran off the stage.

It took me about thirty minutes to make my way through the crowd. I guess a lot of people saw the kiss because they screamed, "You go, girl!" when I passed.

I finally made it outside to the limousine. Rachel was already there and she was freaking out! She jumped up and down and said she'd caught the kiss on her camera!

"You should have seen the look on Regan's face," Rachel said. "Camy, it was priceless. I wish I had taken a picture of her, too!"

To tell you the truth, I didn't know how to feel. I had never won a bet like that before. I think I was still a little dazed. "Where *is* Regan?" I asked. "She should've been here by now."

It was about a half hour later when we realized Regan wasn't coming back to the limousine. Our driver was really worried. He frantically called the hotel and found out that Regan had called her father to pick her up and was already in her room.

Regan must have been really mad to just leave like that. Or maybe she was too embarrassed to face us.

Or maybe it had really, really disappointed her to lose the bet to me—Ms. Modest.

be open with your feelings

Jackie always shares her feelings with me. If she's feeling mad, happy, sad, frightened, nervous, or tense, I know about it. And the same is true for me. We share everything. And sharing our feelings makes our friendship stronger.

But some girls have a hard time opening up to people. And that's okay!

If you have a hard time expressing your feelings to a friend, it might be because you 're afraid your friend won't understand.

Trust is a *big* part of opening up to a friend. It might seem like a risk to share your feelings, especially if you've never done it before. Your friend could laugh at you, tell you you're crazy, and never talk to you again!

Chances are, though, your friend will be very supportive and understanding. You'll probably discover that your friend has had *very* similar feelings to yours.

But if you never share your feelings, how will you ever realize that other people have similar feelings too?

The best thing about opening up is that you're giving your friend the chance to *understand* you. It's very wonderful to know there is a person in this big, crazy world of ours who actually understands you.

Sharing your feelings is addictive, it really is. Once you find the person you trust to open up to, you'll do it all the time. And you'll feel so much better.

So share your feelings with a friend you trust. I *guarantee* you'll like it! ☺

15

keep a secret

in the previous rule, I talked about the importance of sharing your feelings.

A *really* common way to reveal your feelings is through a secret. For instance, maybe you tell your friend that you like a particular boy. With this secret, you're sharing your feelings only with your friend, and no one else knows.

Telling secrets is a great way to develop trust. You tell a friend a secret; then she tells you a secret. Now you have a really special bond.

When I tell Jackie a secret, I'm telling her something I don't want anyone else to know.

83

And I know she'll keep it a secret. I totally trust her. Because Jackie realizes that if she *didn't* keep my secrets, I would stop telling her things about me. And if she didn't know anything about me, how could we ever be really good friends?

So secrets come with a *lot* of responsibility.

Just remember: It's a privilege to know your friend's secret. She has chosen to reveal something about herself that she hasn't told anyone else!

Sometimes you might be tempted to tell someone else your friend's secret. Maybe you have another friend you hang out with, and you're just dying to tell her!

Or maybe you *accidentally* tell someone else your friend's secret. Maybe you think the secret isn't that important and your friend won't be upset if you tell it to someone else.

Well, think about how your friend might react if she found out you told her secret. It might really hurt her feelings to find out you broke her trust. I mean, you wouldn't want her to tell *your* secrets, would you?

So really, by keeping secrets, you're telling your friend she can always trust you. And you should *never* do anything to break this special bond.

There is an important exception to this rule, however, which takes me to my *next* rule. I hope, I hope, I hope you *never* have to use rule #16:

if it's a *big* secret, tell an adult

16

no one has ever come to me with a *really* big secret. Like they purge after eating. Or they're being sexually abused. Or they've started doing drugs.

I've often wondered what I would do if someone ever did tell me something really big.

I decided that if a friend ever told me a *really* big secret, I would probably tell my mom.

But what makes a secret really big? How exactly would I know if I had to break my friend's trust and tell her secret, even if she made me promise not to?

I asked my mom's advice on this one. She

understood my dilemma. My mom said there were three important things to consider when deciding if I *had* to tell the secret. She suggested I ask myself the following questions:

1. Can I get into trouble by knowing this secret and not telling anyone?

2. Do I feel really unsafe by knowing this secret?

3. Am I, is my friend, or is anyone else in *physical danger* if I don't tell this secret?

Even if a friend makes you swear you will never tell anyone, if the secret is really, *really* big and you answer yes to one or more of the above questions, you *have* to break your promise and tell an adult—a teacher, your parents, a counselor, etc.

It will be a *very* difficult thing to reveal your friend's secret. Your friend might find out. She might feel betrayed. She might never talk to you again!

But ask yourself this: "What would happen if I *didn't* reveal the secret?" If something bad happened to you or your friend because you didn't tell the secret, wouldn't you feel even *worse*?

Now pretend for a moment your friend tells you she's doing something that could get her into trouble. You wonder if you should tell an adult. So you ask yourself the questions on the previous page and find:

1. *You* won't get into trouble for knowing what your friend is doing.

2. You don't feel unsafe by knowing what she is doing.

3. You, your friend, or anyone else are not in physical danger because of what she's doing.

But your friend *could* get into trouble. Should you still go to an adult and tell what your friend is doing?

I again asked my mom about this one. She said I should always use my best judgment. She said I'll know in my heart if I need to tell her.

But she also encouraged me to use the next rule:

17

let them make their own mistakes

Sometimes a friend will tell you she's doing things you don't approve of. Like shoplifting. Or maybe she's going out with a boy you think is trouble. You've heard bad stories about this guy, but your friend doesn't want to listen. What do you do? Do you:

1. Tell on her?

2. Quit being her friend?

3. Give her advice and hope she listens?

This is a very difficult question, but #3 is normally the correct answer.

While she might get into trouble for shop-lifting, she isn't really in physical danger.

And you should not necessarily stop being her friend just because she's going out with a boy you don't like.

In both cases, you simply need to give her advice and then let her come to her own decision.

Your friends will occasionally make mistakes. So will you. We all do! Lord knows, *I've* made tons of mistakes!

When we make mistakes, though, we usually learn from them. Learning from our mistakes helps us grow. After we make a mistake once, hopefully we won't make the same mistake again. So mistakes might be painful, but they are necessary.

It is only natural for you not to want to see your friend get into trouble. And maybe you really do know what's best for her. So you should give your friend good advice. The thing is, you can't *force* her to follow your advice. Your friend has to make her own decisions. Maybe she *needs* to learn her lesson the hard way.

There's one last thing to consider about this rule.

Jackie is a very smart girl who doesn't get into a lot of trouble. But what if she were the type of person who always made mistakes or bad choices? For instance, what if Jackie were *always* going out with the wrong kind of guy? Or continually shoplifted?

It would be very painful for me to watch her constantly make bad choices about her life. Not only would it be painful, but her bad choices could one day rub off on *me*.

Again I remind you, Jackie is not like this at all. But if she *were* the kind of friend who continually made bad choices that got her into trouble, I would have to consider ending the friendship.

After all, I couldn't let my friend's bad choices and mistakes ruin *her* life and *mine*, could I?

don't start nasty rumors—
ever!

in the second grade at Beverly Hills Elementary, there was this really hurtful rumor floating around about me. Since my dad worked for the electric company, some kids were saying that if you touched me, you would be electrocuted.

One boy threw a pencil at me to see if it would spark. Of course it didn't spark. I told on the boy and he had to go to the principal!

Another rumor about me when I lived in Beverly Hills was started by Regan. Because I wore funky, cool thrift store shoes, Regan started saying that my dad was an undertaker and I stole the shoes off dead people! That rumor went *no*where. Everyone already knew my dad was an electrician.

This rule is important because it's harder to make friends, and keep friends, if people know you as the type of girl who starts or spreads rumors.

So how do nasty rumors start? Usually with a whisper.

I'm sure you've seen this type of girl before: She's always whispering into her best friend's ear. It's like they're stuck together with glue! Then the friend listening to the whisper will look up, gaze around the room, and laugh.

Of course these two girls are talking about someone. And you pray it isn't *you*!!! These girls could be telling secrets about another girl, but more than likely they're talking bad about her. They're spreading a rumor.

Rumors are started for a bunch of different reasons: #1—misunderstanding; #2—jealousy; #3—cruelty; #4—revenge.

Whatever the reason may be, you are not being a nice person if you spread a rumor. Even if you didn't start the rumor, by passing it along, you're still intentionally hurting someone.

Our reputations are very important. And

nasty rumors hurt our reputations. And if you hurt someone's reputation, you are hurting them.

I mentioned earlier in the book that Jackie's ex-boyfriend started a rumor that I was a Beverly Hills snob. (Yes, even boys spread rumors!) Rather than get upset about it, I laughed. Because *I* know who I am. What I think about myself is more important than what others think of me.

But recently I heard another, more harmful rumor about me. Since I have never had a boyfriend at Peoria Middle School, there was a rumor that I was dating a high-school guy.

That rumor bothered me. But instead of reacting to it, I reminded myself that *I* knew the truth about myself, and no one else's opinion could hurt me unless I let it.

My point is, if a rumor is ever spread about you, try to ignore it. Most rumors die down pretty quickly anyway.

But if the rumor is *really* bad and people start making fun of you, I recommend telling a teacher or an adult you trust. They might be able to intervene and get the rumor stopped.

In the end I think we just need to remember this: We should always treat other people the way we want to be treated ourselves. *That* is what respect is all about.

So if you don't want nasty rumors spread about yourself, then don't spread them about *others*!

a bet in maui—part 3

the day after the concert and my victory, Rachel woke me up earlier than usual. "So what should we do today," she said, pausing for effect, "*without* Regan!!!!"

"Rachel, I think I did something really bad."

"What do you mean? You won the bet! We don't have to see her for the rest of our lives! I, for one, am happy about that."

"First of all, your parents could get married, so you might be seeing her on Thanksgiving, Christmas, and possibly New Year's. Or worse! You guys might have to live together—"

Rachel stopped me cold. "It's too horrible to imagine."

"Seriously, I feel *really* bad."

"Why?"

"I don't know."

"What are you going to do?"

"I just need some time to think about it."

Rachel was disappointed, but she's a great friend and knows when to give me space. She said, "I for one am not about to let this beautiful day go to waste. Come out to the pool later, okay?"

I said okay, then got dressed.

Before I knew it, I was at the door to Regan's suite. I knocked, and Regan's father opened the door. "Camy, pleasant surprise. You're up early!"

"I know, I'm sorry to bother you. . . ."

"I think Regan's still asleep, but I could wake her—"

"No, no, that's okay I'll see her later."

From the next room I heard Regan call loudly: "I'm awake."

"Well, go on in. I'm headed down for breakfast. You two join me later."

I said okay, watching nervously as he exited the suite and closed the door, leaving me trapped inside.

Their suite was just like ours, though two

floors below. I walked toward the room I knew was Regan's. I knocked, then entered. Regan was lying in bed with the covers pulled up to her chin. She stared blankly at the wall. She was a mess. It looked like she'd been crying and hadn't slept all night.

"What do you want?" she asked angrily.

"I . . . I just . . ."

"If you're here to gloat, I'm not interested. I saw it, okay? You can go."

"I'm not here to gloat."

"Then what are you here for?"

"To say I'm sorry."

Surprised, Regan dropped the blanket she was holding around her neck. I could see she was still wearing the red dress. She had slept in it.

"It wasn't fair of me to make that bet. I mean . . . it was a stupid bet and I—I don't want you to think . . . ," I stammered.

"Forget it. If *I'd* won, you'd be wearing that T-shirt," she said rudely.

"I know." I sat on the edge of the bed. She didn't tell me to go, so I assumed she wanted me to stay. "I don't want your feelings to be hurt."

"Yeah, right, like you could hurt my feelings.

Who do you think you are, Camy Baker? You mean nothing to me. You've *never* meant anything to me. To think I want to be your and Rachel's friend is a case of mass delusion. So just go!"

She turned away from me. I knew she didn't want me to go, but she always had to try and hurt me. It burned me up. "Fine," I said. I stormed to the bedroom door.

She yelled, "Take this and shove it." I felt something soft hit my back. I turned around and on the floor was a T-shirt. "I'm sure you'll enjoy burning it," she added.

I picked up the T-shirt. On it were the words "Regan is the prettiest, smartest, most fabulous girl in the whole world." It was the shirt I was supposed to wear for losing the bet. I was so mad, I was trembling.

"You can *go*," she said rudely. "You're dismissed."

Tears started pouring down my cheeks. I threw the shirt back at her. "Why do you need me to wear this?!" I yelled. "Do you need someone to tell you you're pretty, intelligent, and fabulous because you don't believe it yourself? Is that it?"

Regan jumped out of bed, shocked and angry at my sudden outburst. "Just get out of here. I'm sick of looking at you!"

"Say more mean things, Regan. Come on, *say* them! You can't hurt me anymore. I'm not going to waste my energy hating you!"

Tears filled her eyes. "Just shut up and get out of here!"

"No! What's the matter, Regan? Are you afraid to cry? Huh? Are you afraid to lose control? Well, you don't have any control over me anymore. I can guarantee you that!"

"Get out of my room!" She was sobbing now. "I *hate* you!"

"You don't hate anybody but *yourself*," I yelled.

Regan dropped to the bed, still sobbing. She put her hands over her face. She screamed, "I hate *everyone*!"

I didn't know what to do. Part of me wanted to leave that room, forget about Regan, and get on with my life. Chances are, I would never have to see her again if I didn't want to.

But the other part of me said that Regan was crying out for help and I might just be able to help her. If a person she constantly ridi-

culed could forgive her, maybe she could forgive herself.

I slowly moved to the bed. Regan was crying so hard.

This was such a tough situation. I felt so angry with her, but I also felt sorry for her. I didn't
know whether to hit her or hug her. I finally
knelt down near the bed.

"Regan, it's okay. I'm sorry," I said.

Regan looked up. Her mascara was smeared,
her face was red, and she looked a little wild. "I
just don't want to hate you anymore, Camy."

"I don't want to hate you either." I put my
arms around her shoulders.

Regan hugged me back. And when she did, I
knew she was never going to push me away
again. Something very painful for both of us
was ending. Kneeling there in Regan's room,
with both of us sobbing, I knew one of my former enemies had just become a friend.

And it felt good. *Really* good.

THE END

find something good about someone you don't like

there are some girls who just don't like each other. They have what my mom calls personality clashes. For instance, Regan and I. We totally had a personality clash.

I really didn't like the way she bossed other girls around. Or tried to control other girls by making fun of them if they didn't do what she wanted them to do. Like the way she made fun of me because I didn't wear those really expensive clothes that she and her friends wore.

On the flip side, Regan thought I talked too much. She thought I was fake because I was always so bubbly, as she put it.

After our breakthrough in Maui, we spent a

lot of time talking. We discussed our differences. After we got them out in the open, we realized how much we'd misunderstood each other.

Finally I said to Regan, "Maybe we should have focused on what we *liked* about each other, rather than what we disliked. We could have been friends *years* ago!"

The point of this rule is that you might know a girl you simply do not like. But rather than make fun of her, be mean to her, or spread rumors about her, why don't you instead turn all that negative energy into something positive? Why not think of something nice about her?

For instance, with Regan, I could have focused on how smart she is. Or how she's a natural leader and other girls look up to her. Or that she really loves her parents. Those are all really great qualities.

I'm not saying that if there's a girl you don't like, you *have* to become friends with her. But why waste the energy hating her?

It's like that line from that really awesome movie *Waiting to Exhale:* "If you're ugly inside, you're ugly outside."

What this means is that no matter how pretty or how well dressed you are, if you have a bad attitude, people aren't going to be attracted to you as a person.

And if people are not attracted to you as a person, why would they want to become your friend?

Thinking good thoughts about someone you don't necessarily like is going to help you become a better person. And as a better person, you'll be just as pretty on the inside as you are on the outside!

So think positive thoughts about someone you don't like. And who knows? Maybe you'll even start *liking* her! ☺

20
if a friend bothers you, it's okay to tell her

I mentioned in the previous rule that it's always important to look for the best qualities in a person. But there might come a time when a friend really gets on your nerves. And that's okay!

Friends can make us mad or hurt or annoyed in many ways. But unless you *tell* your friend you're mad or hurt or annoyed, she'll never know! And she'll most likely keep doing the thing that bothers you until you finally have to scream at her!

Let's use an example. Say you have a friend who smacks her lips whenever she eats. Like

105

real loud. It's totally gross and kind of makes you sick to your stomach. It *really* annoys you. Finally you just can't take it anymore. You scream, "Chew with your mouth closed, it's totally grossing me out!"

If you approach the situation this way, don't you think your friend will be totally offended? Especially if someone else hears you scream at her? She'll be embarrassed.

But sometimes you have to risk hurting a friend's feelings to make things right. And you can't expect your friend *not* to be a little hurt or angry when you bring up something about her that's bothering you.

A really good way to approach this, though, is to wait until you two are alone. Then you could say: "Can we talk about something? I'm kind of having a problem. I know it might hurt your feelings, but I have to tell you because I don't want to stop being your friend just because of this problem."

See how that would work? You've told your friend you have a problem and it's really bothering you, but you're willing to work it out.

Next you could say: "We eat together a lot.

Every day at lunch. And when you eat, you chew with your mouth open. And it's kind of annoying."

Your friend could get really defensive and say you're the one with the problem, not her. No one likes to be told they aren't perfect. But chances are, if you present your problem to her in a calm, clear, nonaccusing way, she'll listen to you and will try to work things out.

The point of this rule is that a friendship is a fifty-fifty relationship. Not a seventy-thirty relationship, where one person has more control than the other.

But an *equal* relationship. You should always be able to tell your friend how you feel. And your friend should always be able to tell you how she feels. If you have a problem, or she does, you should try to work it out calmly. You do that by (a) admitting there is a problem, and (b) talking about it.

If you don't admit there is a problem, and you don't talk about it, then the problem could keep growing and growing until there's this huge shouting match and one of you starts crying.

But ask yourself this: Wouldn't it have been easier just to work out the problem when it first came up? After all, life without tears of frustration and screams of rage is much nicer. Trust me on this one! ☺

21

be a leader, not a follower

being a leader doesn't necessarily mean ruling over other people. A true leader is a person who sets a good example, cooperates with others, and works to make sure everyone in her group feels safe, secure, and happy.

With that in mind, I have a test for you.

You can become friends with *one* of the girls listed below, but you can't become friends with both. You have to choose between Girl #1 and Girl #2:

Girl #1 is the envy of all the girls, and every boy wants to go out with her. (Just for the record, this is my definition of the old-fashioned kind of popularity.) This girl promises to be your best friend. But she is very particular about certain things. For instance, you can't say anything that might make her or you look stupid.

If she thinks you need to dress differently, you agree to dress differently. Or if she thinks you need to stop a certain friendship because in her opinion the girl is a geek, you stop the friendship.

By being friends with Girl #1, you get to be popular in the old-fashioned way.

Girl #2 is well liked in your school. She already has a best friend, so you would be just a regular friend. Girl #2 is very friendly, and she likes you just the way you are.

Being friends with Girl #2 means you'll always have people to each lunch with. And you'll always be invited to whatever activity is going on in the group.

But by becoming this girl's friend, nothing *really* dramatic happens in your life.

If you chose Girl #2, then you are 1000% correct.

The difference between Girl #1 and Girl #2 is *you*. Because with Girl #1—the really "popular" girl who you think can make all your dreams come true—to become popular, you have to change. You have to become Girl #1's follower. You have to go from being a smart, wonderful, great person to being a person who is told what to do, when to do it, and how to do it.

A true friend always accepts you for who you are. And if you're being a true friend, then you accept your friend for who *she* is.

With Girl #2, not a lot happens to you. But the point is: *Not a lot happens to you!!!* You don't have to suddenly become something you aren't! You don't have to change your way of talking or dressing, which ultimately affects your way of thinking. You get to be *you*.

Girl #2 is part of a team. Each girl on that team is individual and powerful in her own right. Together, they form a stronger unit. Now *that's* GIRL POWER!

So not being a follower means always remembering who *you* are. When you remember who you are, then nobody can make you do anything you don't want to do.

And the *best* way to stay true to who you are is to use my next rule:

22
learn the power of the word *no*

yes is a very easy word to say. Sometimes it's easier to go along with what everyone else is doing, saying, or wearing.

When you say no, you're saying, "I'm not like that." Or "I don't do that." You're setting and following your own limits and boundaries.

Some kids think that if you say no, something must be wrong with *you*.

HELLOOOOOO!

No is a *very* courageous thing to say! In this crazy world of ours, *no* is one of the only words that give us any power at all!

When you say no, you are saying that you don't agree with what is happening and will not follow along. It reinforces the fact that you know you are individual, special, and unique— and you will not compromise that. Not now. Not *ever*!

I've said before that at the root of any good friendship are care, trust, and respect. Well, where do these things originate but within you?

And saying no to situations or things you know aren't good for you means you respect yourself, trust your own judgment, and care about your safety.

Start to use the word *no* now! If you don't, you might forget to use it later.

And who knows? If you say no now, you might save a friendship, your self-respect . . . or your *life*!

23

it takes a confident and mature person to apologize

i mentioned earlier that it's perfectly natural to have fights with your friend. And in most fights, it's obvious who is at fault. Like that huge fight I had with Jackie. She blew up at me for no reason. But Jackie did the right thing by apologizing and buying me a new tape recorder.

A lot of times, though, fights happen between friends and it's not clear *who* is at fault.

Let me give you an example. Say, for instance, there's a particular boy you like. And you see your best friend flirting with the boy at lunch one day. Later you confront your friend and tell her she better stay away from the boy.

114

And your friend tells you that you're *totally* overreacting. And then you both start shouting at each other, and it leads to a huge blowout.

Now, maybe your friend *was* flirting with the guy, and it really hurt your feelings. So in a way you had every reason to be mad at her. But maybe she does have a point: You *could* be overreacting.

I have seen a lot of these kinds of fights between friends—where it isn't really clear who exactly is at fault. These kinds of fights are the worst.

In some cases, friends *never* make up. They totally quit talking to each other! And as time passes, the two former friends become bitter enemies!

Everything could be patched up if one friend would apologize. But what happens when each thinks the other person should apologize?

I'll tell you what happens. They both become stubborn. Since each thinks the other person is at fault, *neither* girl ends up apologizing at all!

If this ever happens to you, I suggest you sit down and think about the reason you and your friend got into a fight. And be honest with yourself. Was the fight even partly your fault? Maybe not all your fault, but a *little* bit?

You'll find that most of the time, *both* friends are partly responsible in a fight. And if you can be honest enough with yourself and admit you're at least partly responsible, then I truly believe you should apologize to your friend. Even if you think she started it. Even if you think she's more responsible for the fight than you.

Now, I'm not meaning to say you have to take all the blame. Your friend should apologize too. But why not be the one to apologize first?

As my dad always says, "It takes a confident and mature person to apologize." What that means is when you apologize, you're showing your friend that you're confident and mature enough to accept your responsibility for the fight. Not only will your friend probably appreciate your confidence and maturity, but *you* will feel better about *yourself*! Why? Because instead of holding a grudge toward your friend, you're taking steps to clear the air.

And even if your friend doesn't accept your apology—or refuses to apologize to you in return—you'll know that you gave it your best effort to save the friendship.

In my experience, though, I've found that if you make the first move and own up to your share of the blame, your friend will apologize too. Hopefully, you can then be friends again! ☺

24
try not to be controlling
of your friends

Let's face it. Our friends have more influence on us than anyone else. And when a friend says something about us that is negative, we're *devastated*!

Why would a friend do this? Why would she criticize our hair, our clothes, or our choices in boyfriends?

A friend might say something negative in an effort to control our behavior. If you're doing something she doesn't approve of, she might say something negative to pressure you into making a different choice.

In short, she's being controlling.

If you're the kind of girl who constantly tries

to control people, the thing you need to realize is that you're not in an open and honest relationship. You're in a one-sided relationship. Sure, you might be dominating a person for your own needs, but is the friendship healthy? I don't *think* so.

To better explain this rule, I went to an expert. And that person was none other than my former enemy, Regan.

After our breakthrough in Maui, I asked Regan to send me her thoughts on why it wasn't good to control people.

She sent me the following e-mail.

Hey, girls!

My name is Regan, and I'm what you might call an expert on being a control freak. I used to go to Beverly Hills Elementary, and I admit I tried to control everyone around me.

When I was in control I felt like *nothing* could hurt me. I didn't have to hear, see, or think about anything I didn't want to hear, see, or think about. I felt powerful.

The incident with Camy helped me see that the old way wasn't working anymore.

In elementary school I never had a close friend

unless I controlled her thoughts, actions, behavior, schedule, friendships, alliances, and comments.

Some girls I could control more than others. For instance, in fifth grade I made a certain girl I will call Nancy my secretary. Nancy took care of my address book as well as all my scheduling. She'd make all my appointments—hair, nails, massage, tennis lessons, etc.

I controlled everything Nancy did. Do I really think she was a *friend*? I suppose in some twisted way I did. But we never talked unless I was telling her what to do!

Nancy wasn't the only girl I controlled at Beverly Hills Elementary. I controlled other girls in different ways. When I started wearing the clothes of a new designer, you can bet almost *every* girl started wearing that same designer. If I got a new cell phone, that phone suddenly became very popular.

Camy was about the only girl at Beverly Hills Elementary I couldn't control. (I was never interested in controlling Rachel. She just didn't care what was going on at school, not in the same way Camy did.)

I have to admit, though, it became a mission for me to sabotage Camy. Because if a girl can't be *controlled,* she must be *sabotaged*!!!

Everything that happened in Maui, though,

taught me something. After I cried—which I *never* do—I realized how much energy it was taking to hate Camy Baker.

After we decided to be friends, it was so much easier! I didn't have to spend all my time plotting and scheming to sabotage her. It never worked anyway.

In Maui, Camy told me she wanted our friendship to be equal and special. For us to achieve this, she set up a bunch of rules. (Camy really *is* big on rules!)

Like if we had a problem with each other, we should talk about it. And we should always be considerate of each other's feelings. Really simple stuff when you think about it, but these things were, like, totally foreign to me. I told her I would give it my best effort.

Anyway, it takes a lot of energy to be controlling. SO DON'T DO IT! J.k.—as Camy would say.

So that's it. See ya!!!

P.S. Camy:
That's all I have to say about the rule. I hope I explained it right. Does it make sense? Does this e-mail sound evil? If it does, you can change it. You're the writer, not me, so go ahead and make any corrections.

By the way, I got the new BoyzLife CD and it *rocks*. Have you heard it?

Not much else is new in Beverly Hills. My dad's still seeing *(name deleted for privacy)*. It looks *really* serious. Maybe Rachel and I will be stepsisters after all. She'll just die! Don't tell her I said that!

Call me if you need more information for the rule. Gotta go! Love You Like a Sister! (or LYLAS for short!)

Regan

CAMY'S NOTE:

I am very proud of Regan for admitting that the negative way she used to treat people was actually hurting *her*. It takes a very courageous person to admit that. My only hope for Regan now is that she sticks with it and develops friendships that are open and honest, and take into account her friend's feelings.

I have faith in Regan. I know she can do it. And if you see yourself in the type of girl Regan describes, I know you can be a better friend, too. All you have to do is try! ☺

25

choose your friends carefully

regan mentioned in the previous rule she would only become friends with a girl she could control. She explained why she chose her friends this way. She felt powerful.

If you're the kind of girl who would be friends with someone like Regan, you need to ask yourself *why* you would let a friend control you? Why would you go from being a smart and fabulous girl to one who doesn't think, act, or speak without somebody's permission?

Or for that matter, why would you continue a friendship if you really don't like the girl?

Or why would you continue a friendship

123

simply because your friend lets you borrow her clothes?

Or why would you continue a friendship if your friend totally bores you? Or uses you? Or makes fun of you? Or never supports you? Or puts you down in front of others? Or tells your secrets? Or steals your boyfriends?

If you're in a friendship like any of those I described above, you need to wake up and smell the CK One! And if you tend to choose people who don't care for, trust, or respect you, you need to take more time picking your friends! I mean, come one! Some girls spend more time deciding what to wear in the morning than deciding which girls they should be friends with!

When you get involved in a friendship, you're making a choice. You're *choosing* to be in that friendship. Nobody is forcing you into it.

Sometimes we won't know for a while whether we made the right choice when we choose a particular friend. And that's okay. Sometimes it takes a while to *really* get to know someone. If after a few weeks into the friendship, though, you realize this girl isn't good for you, you should distance yourself from the relationship.

The most important thing I hope you've gotten out of my book so far is that friendships are very wonderful relationships. The best! But friendships just don't happen without effort.

Friendships take work. They take commitment. They take time, and they take honesty. Honesty with your friends, and honesty with yourself. You'll know, deep down, if your friendship is working for you.

And how will you *really* know if you've made a good choice in friends and your friendship is working for you? Easy.

Having this friendship makes you feel better about *yourself*.

26

let go when you have to

We've all had a friend who at one time is *the* best friend we've ever had. Life without this friend is unimaginable!

Then something really strange happens. You feel like you and your best, most greatest friend have drifted apart. You feel like you don't really *know* this person anymore.

This is confusing. It is also frightening. How could you be such great friends one minute, then the next minute barely talk?

This rule addresses the painful fact that sometimes friends just grow apart.

My friend Brie had an experience to share that summed up this rule perfectly. I talked to Brie, who lives in Beverly Hills, over the phone.

CAMY: So, Brie, what does this rule mean?

BRIE: Well, you know Kris and I had been best friends since third grade.

CAMY: We used to call you the Bobbsey Twins. Those matching outfits were great!

BRIE: That *was* the fourth grade—we grew out of it. Anyway . . . Kris and I are no longer best friends.

CAMY: I heard. *What* happened?

BRIE: Well, that's why I came up with this rule. There really isn't any reason. See, over the summer before sixth grade, after you left, Kris and I hung out as usual and stuff, but . . . it just got to be boring. Like we had already done *everything* we could possibly do together, you know?

And, um, well—I guess we were both nervous about starting sixth and stuff, and it was like we were getting on each other's nerves. Nothing too bad, but it was like—okay, we need a break. . . .

CAMY: *Nothing* happened?

BRIE: I swear, nothing. I mean, we just stopped calling each other, you know? It's just—well, I love to shop. I like to hang out on Melrose and stuff, but Kris never wanted to. Kris likes watching TV. And if I had to sit through another *Real World,* I was going to . . .

CAMY: I feel your pain.

BRIE: Anyway, Kris and I don't hang out anymore and there's really no reason for it. So it made me think of this rule. I'll always love her and stuff, but we're just not close. We say hi at school now, but it's different. It's like we don't even know each other. She's dating Chad, you know . . .

CAMY: Get out!

BRIE: No lie.

CAMY: My Lord, what does she see in that boy?

BRIE: I dunno. Anyway, that's my story.

CAMY: By the way, who's paying for this call?

BRIE: You called me, remember?

CAMY: Thanks for the rule. Gotta go!

CAMY'S NOTE:

When a cherished friendship ends, as Brie says, sometimes there is just no reason for it.

You have to remember we're at a point in our lives where we're changing. Our bodies are changing, our minds are changing.

In short, our personalities are changing. It makes sense to me that as we change, our taste in friends changes, too.

If something like this ever happens to you—if you and a former best friend don't seem to have much in common anymore—it's okay!

I do suggest you talk to your former best friend about the situation, just to make sure there are no resentments on either side. If you grow out of the friendship before your friend does, she might be really hurt.

Tell your friend what you're feeling. Just because you're not "best" friends anymore, you can still be friends.

After all, friends are like clothes—you can never have too many! But you certainly want the ones that fit you best!!! ☺

129

27

forget the rules

there are thousands of ways you can make a friend or improve your friendships that I probably have not covered in this book!

Friendships happen. They always do. There are as many different friendships as there are days in the year. That's 365, by the way—except for leap year, which makes it 366.

My older sister, Sara, says that by the time she graduated high school, she had a total of seven best friends throughout her school years.

How did Sara get all those best friends? She didn't have this book to refer to. She just sort of had to make it up as she went along.

I guess my point is, don't pressure yourself to follow all these rules. You'll probably have great friendships without any help from me! Make up or follow your own rules. But if you ever need advice or inspiration, you know who to turn to! ☺

28
have fun!

it can be serious business being a '90s kind of girl. We have a lot of pressure to look, act, and behave a certain way.

Also, our lives can get pretty crazy. We have school, chores, homework. Add a couple of trips to the mall, a few hours a day of television, and we haven't got any time left to *think*! Because of all the things going on in our lives, it's easy to forget the simple moments.

Like a really good laugh. Or the crazy times when a friend does something unexpected. Like stick a flower in her hair. Or spit water through the gap between her teeth.

And sometimes, fun moments can happen when you least expect it. For instance, a funny thing happened to Jackie the other day. We were on our way to the bus stop and Jackie was a little grumpy. Suddenly she tripped and landed right in a big puddle of water! She wasn't hurt or anything, but her clothes were covered with water and mud! And I couldn't help it. I started busting up!

Jackie looked up at me and, for a minute, I thought maybe she was mad. But then she busted up too! When we got to school, she changed into her gym clothes, and we laughed about it all day!

My point is, the most magical moments in our lives are the really small moments. The moments when no one else is looking. The moments with a great friend when you're just being silly and enjoying each other's company.

Also remember that if you ever feel a particular friendship isn't as fun as it used to be, there are *thousands* of things you can do to make it fun again. Try new things! Hang out in new places. Laugh, play, joke, tease!

Don't let your friendship fall into a rut! Don't take life so seriously! Shake things up a bit! After all, maybe your friendship hasn't fallen into a rut. Maybe you've just temporarily forgotten to have fun!

Never underestimate the power of acting young and silly and crazy—but not *too* crazy. You don't want to be carted off to the insane asylum! ☺

29

learn the friendship poem

i mentioned in the previous rule how busy our lives can get. Because we're so busy, it's easy to forget these thirty cool rules for making better friendships.

So to help you remember the rules, I've come up with a friendship poem. This poem doesn't rhyme because I'm working on a new style of poetry—free verse. You should try free verse. It's really fun!

Anyway, it's a really simple poem and it should be easy to memorize. It covers all the basic points of this book. It goes a little something like this:

135

Love You Like a Sister

by Camy Baker

I am here for you.
I will listen to, respect,
and care for you.
My trust
I will give,
your trust
I will receive.
If there is anything
I do not understand
about you
I will try other ways
to understand.
On you,
and our friendship,
I will not give up
without a fight.
Because now that
I know you,
I realize how special
you are to me.
For all these reasons,
and many more,
I love you—
like a sister.

30

the final rule

i wrote something in my journal recently. I asked myself: If I suddenly found a magic lamp and could ask for one wish, what would I wish for?

You might think I would wish for a million dollars. But that's not what I would wish for. You might think I would wish that Brad Pitt was my boyfriend. But that's not what I would wish for either.

I hope you know one thing about me from my books. I hope you understand that I really, really want girls to feel good about themselves. You could say it makes *me* feel good to help girls feel better about themselves.

And if you can feel good about yourself, chances are you're going to have friendships that are really good.

The truth is, my friends, it all starts with *you*. The friendships you have with others are going to be a reflection of what you think about yourself.

If you care for, trust, and respect *you*, you will be better able to care for, trust, and respect others.

If every girl in the world felt good about herself, then maybe all the girls in the world could be friends. And if we felt good about ourselves, we would not try to hurt, compete with, sabotage, or control anyone else. In short if we could *all* be friends, then we could be this great big gang of GIRL POWER. We could rule the world!

And I don't know about you, but I'd like to rule the world! ☺

So if I had a magic lamp, and I only had *one* wish in the world, that wish would be my final rule:

ALWAYS AND FOREVER BE A FRIEND TO YOURSELF.

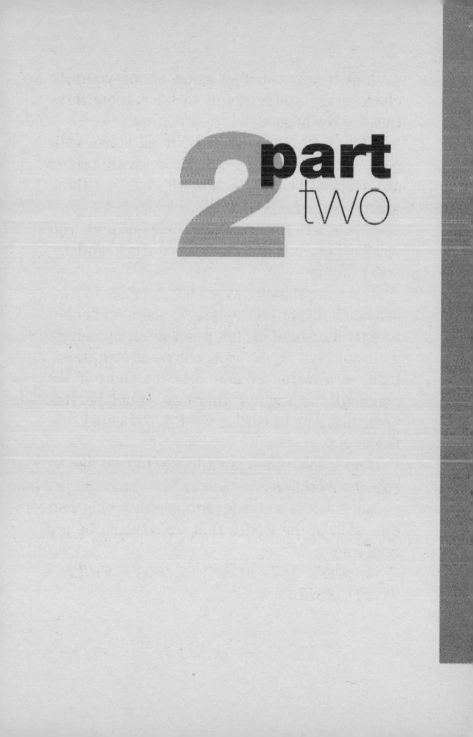

2 part two

q: My best friend told me the other day she likes a guy, who I also like. I haven't told her I like the guy yet. What should I do?

a: You now know from reading rule #10 that I don't think it's a good idea to get into a fight with a friend over a boy. To give you a better understanding of why it's important not to fight over boys, I'll use a shopping story.

Going out with a boy that could end a friendship is like spending fifty dollars for a pair of cool shoes that don't last a month, when you could have bought a sturdy pair of shoes for thirty dollars that would have lasted the whole year! Sure, the fifty-dollar shoes might be in style—for a while—but if they wear out fast, what good are they? When it's cold outside and your feet are freezing, you're going to be very happy you bought the thirty-dollar, sturdy pair of shoes instead!

As for how you should handle this situation with your friend, you should definitely tell her that you like the boy too. Hopefully, together you'll see that your friendship is more important than the boy.

However, there's one more thing to consider. Who does the boy like? If he likes you, hopefully your friend will not be mad if you decide to go out with him. But if he likes her, hopefully you can wish them well and find another boy to get interested in.

Remember, though, there's a very strong chance it will hurt your friendship if one of you starts going out with the boy. I hope you both consider this and realize a friendship is more important than a boyfriend.

q: People in my school make fun of kids who play in the band. I play in the band. It's really embarrassing to be lumped together with all the band kids, who everyone thinks are social retards. Should I quit? And if not, how can I prove I am not a social retard?

a: First of all, I don't like those negative labels. Just because other kids are mean enough to call their peers "social retards" doesn't mean you have to. It sounds like you haven't made any real friends in the band. Why don't you try to get to know them? You'll probably discover that they're very sensitive and talented individuals who have a lot to offer.

Second of all, where do you think some of the most famous musicians got started playing an instrument? In a school band! If you want to be a successful person in life, you have to start somewhere. And if you want to be a musician and start very early—like in the school band—then you're going to be way ahead of the pack!

The question you really need to ask yourself is: Do *you* want to be in the band? Don't let other kids decide for you. Only you can make that decision. If other kids make fun of you for being in a band, then they're the ones with the problem, not you.

Remember this: When you're finally done with school, you'll have the rest of your life. You should always make the choices that are best for the rest of your life!

q: There is this girl in my class whose brother is hot! He's two grades ahead of me, and I'm dying to go out with him. The girl is a complete dork, though. I've tried to become her friend, but she embarrasses me. How do you suggest I get the brother without having to become friends with his sister?

(CAMY'S NOTE TO READERS: I apologize in advance for my answer. It's really brutal. But this girl's question made me very angry.)

a: First of all, I don't like your attitude. You seem to think people are pieces of a puzzle that you can move around as you please. That is *wrong*. Girl, you need to take a good hard look at *yourself*.

You call this boy's sister a total dork who embarrasses you. Have you forgotten that she's a person with feelings? Maybe she isn't as cool

as you obviously think *you* are, but she's probably a much better person than you give her
credit for. If I had a choice between having her
as a friend or you, I would definitely choose
her. You know why? I wouldn't trust you for a
minute.

It makes me *so* angry when kids treat each
other badly. I hope you take a long, hard look at
yourself and realize *you* need to be a lot nicer.

q: I have a friend who always tells my secrets. How can I make her keep a secret for once?

a: As my mom always says, you should never jump to conclusions. Are you sure your friend is the one telling the secret? Maybe you've told someone else who's blabbing?

If you have rock-solid proof this friend is the one telling the secrets, you need to confront her. You need to let her know that your friendship is in *serious* jeopardy. If she's telling your secrets, how can you trust her? And without trust, what good is a friendship?

Explain to your friend how you feel. Let her know how important it is that your secrets *remain* secrets. And if she breaks the secret again, tell her you are *seriously* going to consider ending the friendship.

q: I'm not pretty and I don't dress cool. I think a lot of girls don't want friends who aren't pretty or don't dress cool. Do you have any suggestions?

a: First of all, if someone doesn't want to be your friend because you aren't pretty or you don't dress cool, that's *their* loss.

The thing that bothers me, though, is that *you* say you're not pretty. Pretty is such a hard thing to judge! There are girls in my school who guys think are really hot, but to me they look like Barbie clones with their poufy blond hair. That to me is not pretty.

I think "pretty" is natural and simple. Maybe you need to reconsider if you are pretty or not? And maybe you need to be nicer to yourself?

It could be that *you* are the one assuming other girls don't want to be your friend because of your looks or clothes. They might not be judging you, but you're certainly judging yourself! So chill!

As for your clothes, I'm very sympathetic

about this issue. It's one of the worst things about school, the way everyone is obsessed with clothes. Trust me, in Beverly Hills I was very aware of the fact that my *entire* wardrobe cost less than *one* of Regan's jackets!

Remember this: Some girls can afford fashion. Other girls have to develop their own style. And style is more *attitude* than anything. If you stand tall and hold yourself with confidence, you're going to make an impression on people that a thousand-dollar outfit could *never* make!

q: There's this girl in my Girl Scout troop who is really snotty and mean to me and my two friends in the troop. And guess what? She's vice president. What should I do?

a: Let's hope she reads my books and becomes a nicer person! ☺

Seriously, when someone is mean to you, the first thing you have to realize is that there is nothing wrong with *you*. She's only hurting herself by being a mean person.

But that doesn't mean you have to put up with her insults. You have every right to stand up for yourself. However, I believe it's best to handle the situation in the most mature way possible.

You should never confront a person in a way that could lead to physical fighting. Personally, I believe the best way to handle this situation is to tell the girl that she's *way* out of line, and if she's having a bad day, that's no reason to take it out on *you*.

You know the girl better than I do. Maybe there is some light, funny way you can point out that she's being rude. As my mom says, if you can solve a problem with humor, you are being funny *and* smart. Regardless, let the girl know in your own way that you respect yourself too much to stand for her insults. Chances are, she will stop being snotty and mean to you if she knows you're prepared to stand up for yourself. Best of luck!

q: My friend and I keep getting into fights, and I don't really know what to do about it. Help!

a: As I mentioned before, fights between friends are perfectly natural. But you say you and your friend "keep getting into fights," so it sounds like you have a *lot* of them.

My first question is: Do you know *why* you keep getting into fights? Is there one particular reason? If you can find out that reason, then maybe you can talk to your friend about it. Once the problem is out in the open, maybe you can fix it.

But if you and your friend *constantly* get into fights, and the fights are a result of a personality clash (meaning you and your friend are *so* different that there's a lot of friction), then you might have to consider distancing yourself from the friendship if it's causing you a lot of heartache and anger.

Basically, the question you need to ask yourself is this: Is this friendship more work than fun? I know I've said from the beginning that all friendships take work. But if you're not having any fun (and fights aren't fun!), then maybe it's not the friendship for you.

One last thought: It takes two people to fight. If you and your friend constantly get into fights but you *really* want to save the friendship, then try to be the person who acts more mature. Stop the fight before it gets started, and try and talk it out with your friend.

q: Is it okay to gossip? My mom says it's rude and that I shouldn't do it. But I hear her gossip all the time with her friends! What gives? And why does she say it's rude?

a: The truth of the matter is that it is *very* difficult *not* to gossip. That might explain why your mom gossips even though she tells you not to!

I admit that I like to dish the dirt. (At Peoria Middle School, we call gossiping dishing the dirt. At Beverly Hills Elementary, we called it pouring the tea.) But when I gossip, it's about pretty innocent stuff. I gossip about couples I think will or won't last, who is doing well in school, whose brother I think is cute, etc.

I don't make up gossip, and I certainly try not to gossip about things that might hurt other girls. Gossip is rude only when you're talking badly about someone behind their back or making fun of someone.

So I personally believe that gossip is okay as long as you aren't spreading rumors or saying anything bad about someone else.

q: I'm not impressed with your books. I think you write like a third-grader and the stories you tell are stupid. I feel sad for you, Camy Baker, I really do.

a: This letter was mailed to me by Regan, *way* before we made up in Maui. Of course, she didn't sign the letter. But did she really think I wouldn't figure out who wrote it?! Come on! I'd recognize her chicken-scrawl handwriting anywhere!

final words

Adiòs,
amigas!

I hope you had as much fun reading *Love You Like a Sister* as I had writing it! Not only did I have fun writing this book, I've learned a lot about myself. And I've learned how empty my life would be without my friends! Hopefully, you've learned a few things from the experiences my friends and I have shared too.

Before I go, I want to take this opportunity to thank all the girls who have been e-mailing me their questions and comments! I've been hearing from girls across the country, from California to New York. It's been great hearing from you all, and I hope to get even more fan mail! So, girls, keep it coming!

And if you haven't done so already, check out my Web site: www.camybaker.com.

Anyway, that's all for now, but stay tuned! There are a lot of fun and positive things happening in this wonderfully wacky world of mine! ☺

Peace and love,
Camy Baker

reference

rules at a glance

for easy reference

1. Always and forever cherish your true friends.
2. You'll make friends —there's no need to force it.
3. It's okay to make the first move.
4. Everyone gets rejected once in a while.
5. Conversations are easy— don't be afraid of them.
6. Learn how to listen.
7. Try to have a varied group of friends.
8. It's okay not to have a best friend.

9. It's *okay* to fight.

10. But *don't* fight over boys.

11. Take some time to cool down.

12. Show your friend you care.

13. Don't push too hard.

14. Be open with your feelings.

15. Keep a secret.

16. If it's a *big* secret, tell an adult.

17. Let them make their own mistakes.

18. Don't start nasty rumors—ever.

19. Find something good about
someone you don't like.

20. If a friend bothers you,
it's okay to tell her.

21. Be a leader, not a follower.

22. Learn the power of the word *no*.

23. It takes a confident and
mature person to apologize.

24. Try not to be controlling of
your friends.
25. Choose your friends carefully.
26. Let go when you have to.
27. Forget the rules.
28. Have fun!
29. Learn the friendship poem.
30. Always and forever be a friend
to *yourself*.

and finally, check out

web site
www.camybaker.com

see ya there!!!

bye!